To all of the teachers who supported me and
helped me grow. I am forever grateful.
—J. B. -W.

For Stephen, with all my love x
—S. H.

Published by
PEACHTREE PUBLISHING COMPANY INC.
1700 Chattahoochee Avenue
Atlanta, Georgia 30318-2112
PeachtreeBooks.com

The illustrations were created in Photoshop using layers of
hand painted ink and watercolor textures.

Printed in September 2022 by Toppan Leefung in China
10 9 8 7 6 5 4 3 2 1
First Edition
ISBN: 978-1-68263-166-9

Cataloging-in-Publication Data is available from the
Library of Congress

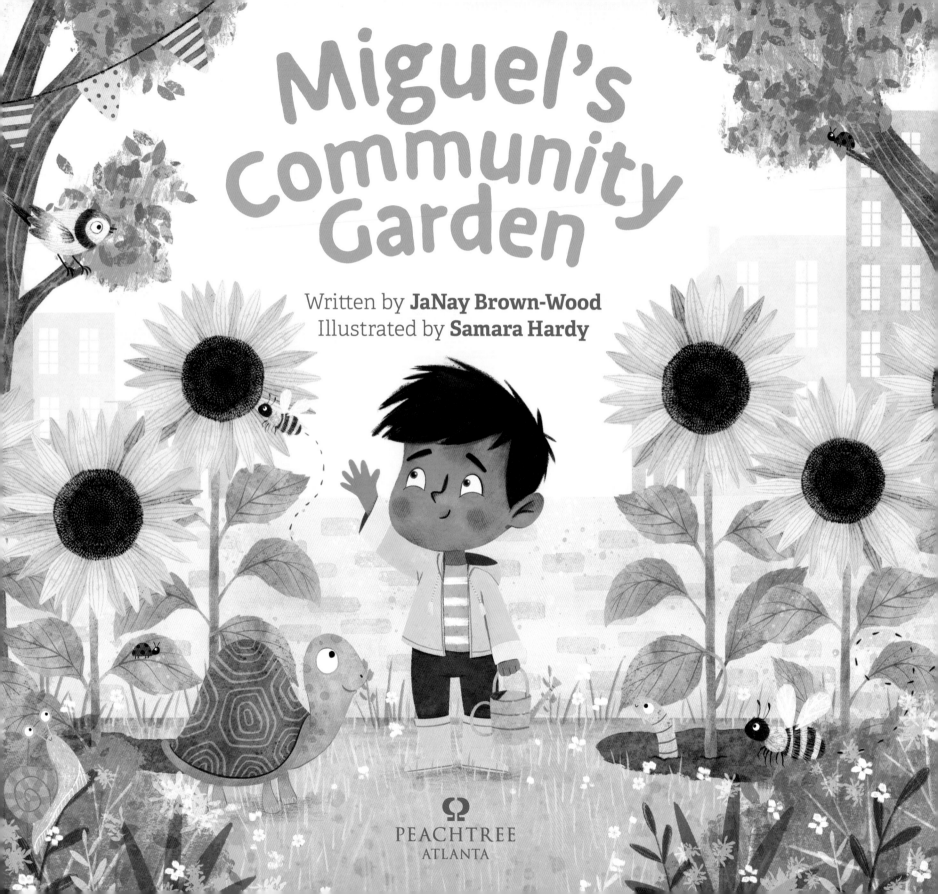

Miguel's Community Garden

Written by **JaNay Brown-Wood**

Illustrated by **Samara Hardy**

PEACHTREE
ATLANTA

Miguel has many plants in his community garden.

Today, Miguel must find his sunflowers for his garden party. What do we know about **sunflowers?**

A sunflower...

is tall.

It has yellow petals
and a round center
with many seeds.

Its leaves are smooth with
pointy tips, and they are
large and stick out.

It also grows from the ground
in the bright sun, and it stands
on a single, thick stem
with its bright flower
on the very top.

Let's help Miguel find his sunflowers!

A **sunflower** is tall.
Is that a **sunflower**?

No. Those are apricots on an apricot tree. An apricot tree is tall, but it is *much* taller than a **sunflower.**

A **sunflower** has yellow petals.
Is that a **sunflower**?

No. Those are artichokes.
An artichoke has petals, but they
are green and not yellow.

A **sunflower** has a round center
that can be seen on the outside.
Is that a **sunflower**?

No. Those are cherries. Cherries do have round centers, but their centers are hidden on the inside.

A **sunflower** has many seeds that are clustered together in its round center. Is that a **sunflower**?

No. Those are mulberries. Mulberries
grow as clusters, but their many seeds
are spread throughout their berries.

A **sunflower** has smooth, green leaves with pointy tips. Is that a **sunflower**?

No. That's spinach. Spinach does have smooth, green leaves, but their tips are usually rounded and not pointy.

A **sunflower** has large leaves
that stick out far from the stem.
Is that a **sunflower**?

No. That's asparagus. Asparagus has
leaf-like scales along its stem, but the
scales are small and do not stick out far.

A **sunflower** grows from the
ground in sunny, bright environments.
Is that a **sunflower**?

No. Those are mushrooms. Mushrooms grow from the ground, but they like cool, wet environments instead of bright sunlight.

A **sunflower** stands on a thick, single stem. Is that a **sunflower**?

No. That's celery. Celery is thick in places, but celery stands with several stalks and not only a single stem.

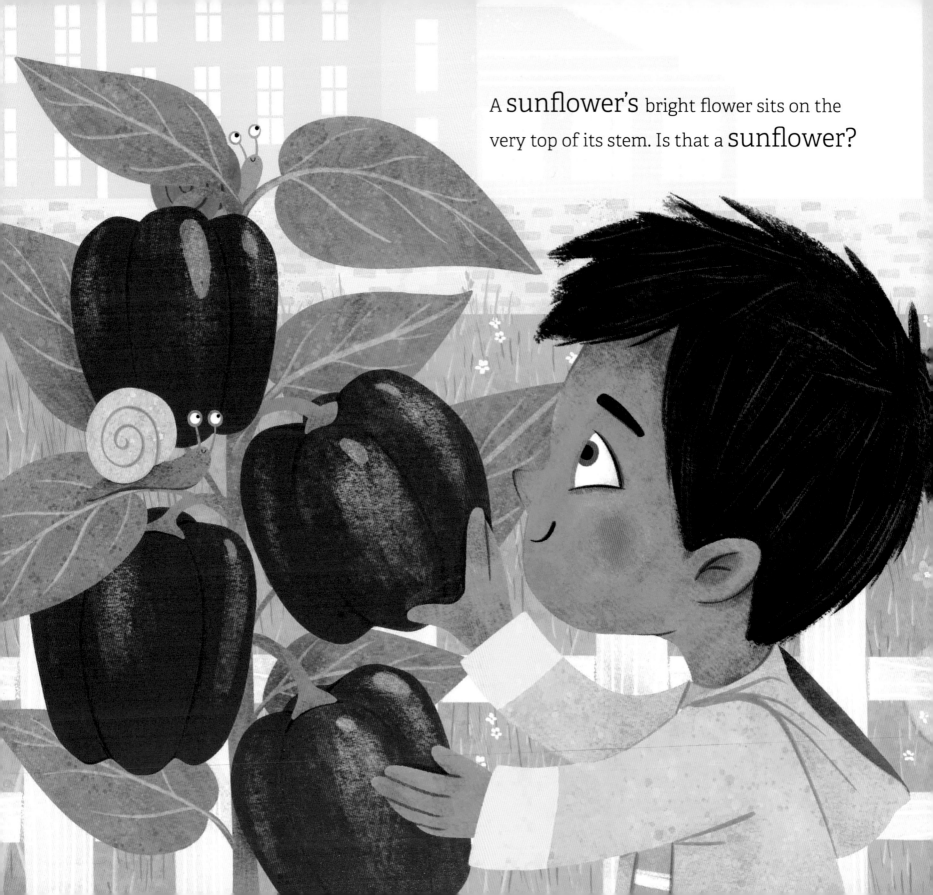

A **sunflower's** bright flower sits on the very top of its stem. Is that a **sunflower**?

No. Those are bell peppers. Bell pepper fruit is bright, but it hangs down from its stem and doesn't sit on top.

Miguel's garden party won't be the same without his **sunflowers**.

We've searched and searched and still no luck!

Where, where, *where* can they be?

Is that a **sunflower**?

Why, yes! That's a **sunflower!**

It's tall and has yellow petals. It has a round center with many seeds clustered together. Its leaves are smooth, green, and pointy, and they are large and stick out far. It grows up from the ground in the bright sun and stands on a thick stem with its bright flower on the very top.

Hooray!

We've found Miguel's **sunflowers.**

And just in time for some wonderful snacks!

Which produce can *you* find at Miguel's garden party?

Sunflower Seed Salad

(Serving size: 2–4)

Ingredients

- 1/2 bunch romaine lettuce
- 3 cups fresh baby spinach
- 1 red or orange bell pepper
- 1 large cucumber
- 1 cup sliced white mushrooms
- 1 cup shelled, roasted, and salted sunflower seeds
- 1 tablespoon lemon or lime juice
- 1 tablespoon olive oil

You'll also need: 1 trusty adult helper

Directions

1. With adult helper's aid, gather ingredients and cooking utensils.
2. Wash all produce in warm water.
3. Have adult helper gather romaine lettuce and cut off stem. Set leaves aside.
4. Break stem off of bell pepper and have adult helper cut in half.
5. Remove bell pepper seeds and ask adult helper to cut pepper into strips, at desired length.
6. Ask adult helper to slice off ends of cucumber and then cut it into half-inch discs. For smaller portions, cut discs into fourths.
7. Measure out spinach and place it into a large bowl.
8. Tear washed romaine lettuce into bite-sized pieces and add to the bowl.
9. Add the bell pepper, cucumber, and mushrooms to the bowl.
10. Toss all the vegetables together using two large spoons.
11. Drizzle one tablespoon of lemon or lime juice and one tablespoon of olive oil to coat the salad.
12. Sprinkle on sunflower seeds.
13. Enjoy!

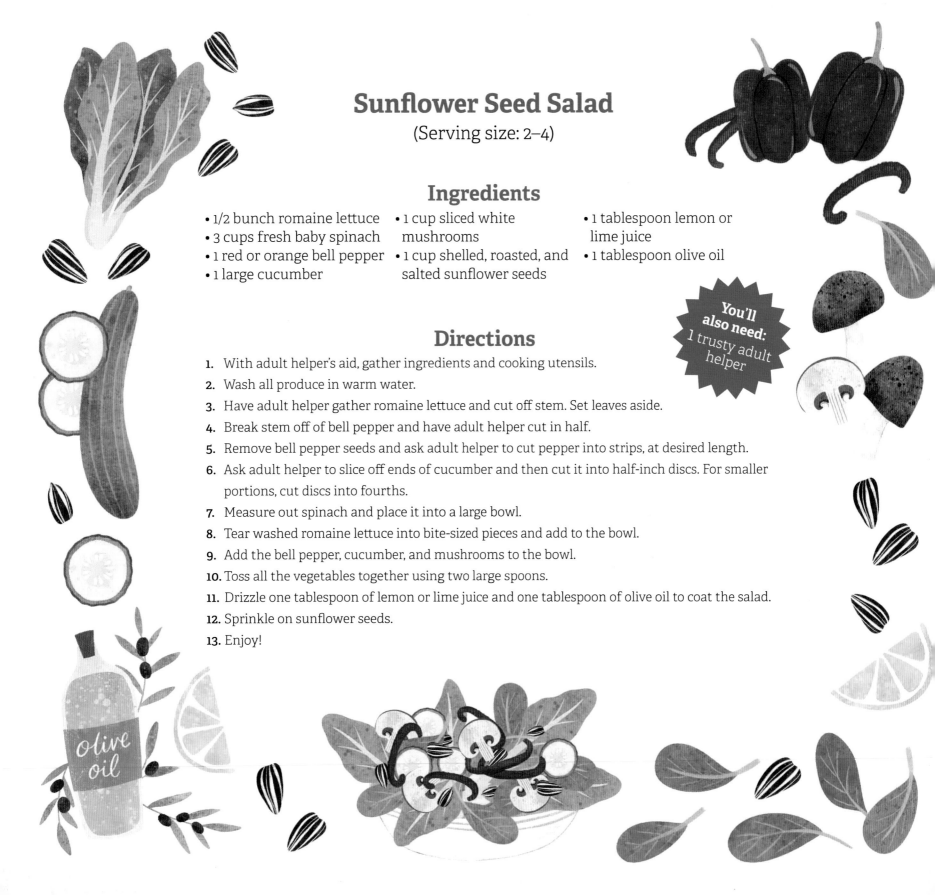